Growing Up Jewish With Sarah Leah Jacobs

My Baby Brother

What a Miracle!

by Sylvia Rouss

Illustrated by Liz Goulet Dubois

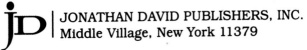

JONATHAN DAVID PUBLISHERS, INC.
Middle Village, New York 11379

To my family and friends,
for their support and encouragement
S.R.

. . .

For Gram
L.G.D.

MY BABY BROTHER
What a Miracle!

Text copyright © 2002 by Sylvia Rouss
Illustrations copyright © 2002 by Jonathan David Publishers, Inc.

Jonathan David Publishers, Inc.
68-22 Eliot Avenue
Middle Village, New York 11379

www.jdbooks.com

2 4 6 8 10 9 7 5 3 1

Library of Congress Cataloging in Publication Data

Rouss, Sylvia A.

My baby brother : what a miracle! / by Sylvia Rouss; illustrated by Liz Goulet Dubois.
  p. cm.
Summary: Sarah does not understand why everyone says that her new baby brother is a
miracle, but then, on the day of his brit (circumcision), she takes another look at him.
  ISBN 0-8246-0445-8
  [1. Brothers and sisters—Fiction. 2. Babies—Fiction. 3.Jews—United States—Fiction.
4.Circumcision—Religious aspects—Fiction. 5. Judaism—Customs and practices—Fiction.]
I. Dubois, Liz Goulet, ill. II. Title.

PZ7.R7622 My 2002

[E]—dc21   2002017517

Text design and composition by John Reinhardt Book Design

Printed in China

Yesterday my baby brother was born.

Today, Daddy took me and my big brother, Aaron, to the hospital to visit Mommy. She was sitting in a rocking chair holding the baby in her arms.

Mommy smiled at me. "Hi, Sarah, I'm so happy to see you!" As I leaned over to give Mommy a kiss, I saw the baby. He was red and wrinkly, with hardly any hair.

"This is your new little brother, Danny," Mommy announced. "Isn't he a wonderful miracle!"

A wonderful miracle? I thought to myself. God created the world in seven days—*that* was a wonderful miracle! My new brother was not a miracle. He wasn't even cute like my neighbor's new puppy. Maybe Mommy had caught something in the hospital that made it hard for her to see.

The next day, we brought Mommy home with the new baby. "Why don't you rest, Deborah?" Daddy suggested to Mommy. "Sarah and Aaron can help me take care of Danny."

The baby began to cry. His face got redder and redder. He opened his mouth. He looked so funny with no teeth!

"I think he's hungry," said Daddy. "Would you like to feed him, Sarah?"

I shook my head no. "Aaron can go first."

Aaron gently took the baby and began giving him a bottle.

"See, Sarah. It's not so difficult." Then he grinned at me and said, "Isn't he a great miracle!"

I looked at the baby's wrinkly face. *A great miracle?* The drop of oil that burned for eight days at Hanukkah—*that* was a great miracle! My new brother was not a miracle! Maybe Aaron had caught Mommy's bad eyesight.

That evening, Bubbie and Zaydie came to our house to visit.

Zaydie's whiskers tickled when he kissed me hello. Bubbie hugged me very tight. "How's the new big sister?" she asked. I just smiled as Mommy picked up the baby so my grandparents could see him.

"Here's your new grandson, Mom and Dad!" she proudly exclaimed. *Oh, no!* I thought. *I hope he doesn't scare them too much.*

Bubbie took one look at the baby and began making funny sounds: "Coo-coo-coo, little one! Coo-coo-coo!" She sounded like a chicken. Then she said, "Sarah Leah Jacobs, he looks just like you when you were a baby!"

Bubbie always says my whole name when she has something really important to say. Maybe she thinks I won't know which Sarah she means. There's a Sarah in the Bible. She's married to Abraham and has a son named Isaac . . . but I don't think her last name is Jacobs.

I ran to look in the mirror. I wasn't bald like Danny! I had brown wavy hair just like Mommy. My face wasn't red and wrinkled. My cheeks were pink, and I had two dimples. I opened my mouth. I had teeth! I did not look like my baby brother! Besides, he's a boy and I'm a big girl!

When Bubbie held Danny, he burped loudly and didn't even say excuse me. Bubbie just laughed. "Sarah, your new little brother is an amazing miracle!"

An amazing miracle? Moses parting the Red Sea—that was an amazing miracle! My new brother was not a miracle! Bubbie already wore glasses. I think she should get a new pair.

The next morning Aunt Judy came to see the baby. She's Mommy's younger sister. Aunt Judy brought a storybook for me and a new outfit for Danny. It looked like pajamas. I would never wear anything like that! Mommy said that as soon as she changed Danny's diaper, he could wear his new clothes.

"I'd be happy to change him," Aunt Judy offered.

I'm happy when I get strawberry ice cream for dessert, but Aunt Judy was happy to change the baby's dirty diaper. Didn't she know it was disgusting? I guess not, 'cause she smiled at me and said, "Isn't he a special miracle, Sarah!"

A *special miracle?* Noah building an ark that could hold two of every kind of animal in the world—*that's* a special miracle! My new brother was not a miracle! Aunt Judy said she had perfect eyesight, but now I wasn't so sure.

Later in the day, our neighbor, Mrs. Weiss, came over to see Danny. Mrs. Weiss just got a new puppy. She named him Mazel, which means "luck." I'm not sure why she calls him that. Mrs. Weiss told Mommy that Mazel had chewed on her slippers, knocked over a flower pot, and had an accident on her carpet.

Mrs. Weiss asked if she could hold Danny. Mommy said yes, and as Mrs. Weiss rocked Danny in her arms, he spit up all over her blouse. *Wow! Is she going to be mad!* I thought.

But Mrs. Weiss just took a cloth from Mommy and wiped her blouse. "A little spit-up never hurt anybody." With a dog like Mazel, I guess Mrs. Weiss felt lucky my brother only spit up on her. Then she said, "Sarah, isn't your new brother a terrific miracle!"

A terrific miracle? Jonah managing to get out of that huge fish—that was a terrific miracle! My new brother was not a miracle.

A few days later, Mommy and Daddy were busy preparing for Danny's *brit*. Mommy explained that Jewish baby boys are circumcised eight days after they are born. When I asked her what that meant, she told me that someone named "Mohel" removes a tiny bit of extra skin. I asked her if it hurt. She said, "Just a little, like when the doctor gives you a shot." I don't like shots, so I'm glad only boys have a *brit*.

I'm glad I'm a girl!

Daddy said that my brother would receive his Hebrew name and become a member of the Jewish people, just like Abraham, the very first Jew. Baby girls receive their Hebrew names when the Torah is read in the synagogue. I was named Sarah Leah, after Daddy's mother.

Lots of family and friends came for Danny's *brit*. I thought, *Now someone will tell my parents the truth about him. He wasn't a miracle.*

As guests gathered around, Mohel said some prayers and did the *brit*. After that, he gave my brother his Hebrew name, Dani'el ben Yosef. Aaron told me that *ben Yosef* means "son of Joseph." Joseph is my daddy's name.

When Danny began crying, Mohel put a drop of wine on his little tongue. I was bored, so I walked over to the table and helped myself to one of Great Aunt Hannah's sprinkle cookies.

Daddy came over. "Sarah, could you please hold the baby for a minute?"

Daddy put Danny on my lap. I looked at his little face. His eyes were closed and his face didn't seem so red anymore. Then, even though he was asleep, Danny smiled!

Aunt Judy said, "He can still taste the sweet wine."

Bubbie said, "He probably has air in his tummy."

Mrs. Weiss said, "It's just a reflex."

His eyelashes look like tiny feathers!

These grownups sure don't know much, I thought. Wine might make Aunt Judy smile, but so will a messy diaper. If Bubbie had air in her tummy, would it make her smile? I don't even know what a reflex is, but it doesn't sound good.

Then I heard Mommy say, "He's smiling because his big sister is holding him."

I thought about all of God's miracles. Then I looked back at Danny's face. He had dimples just like me. He was really cute! I smiled, blinked my eyes to make sure I was seeing okay and realized that everyone was right.

Danny *is* a miracle!